By Jürg Amann & Helga Gebert

Translated by David Henry Wilson

Ten Birds

Read Aloud Rhymes to Bend and Break

NorthSouth
New York / London

TEN fine birds were sitting in a line
When the fence got smashed,
which was not a good sign,
So then there were N I G N.

NINE chirpy birds were singing *Tweet! Tweet!*
When the roof gave way right under their feet,
So then there were E E G H T.

EIGHT hungry birds to diggin' were driven;
But one didn't feel like diggin' for a livin',
So then there were SIVIN.

SEVEN silly birds were twisting in the twigs;
But one got caught in the spiky sprigs,
So then there were SIGS.

SIX scared birds faced trouble and strife
As they squelched through a swamp
in fear of their life,
So then there were FIFE.

FIVE angry birds had a fight about a flower;
But one weak bird just didn't have the power,
So then there were FOUWER.

FOUR playful birds found an egg one day;
But as eggs don't bounce, with eggs you cannot play,
So then there were THRAY.

THREE tired birds were nesting in the straw
When it burst into flames with a terrible roar,
So then there were TWOAR.

TWO lazy birds sat waiting for the sun;
But after a while it wasn't much fun,
So then there was WUN.

Now sing "*Tweet tweet! Tweet tweet!*" and then
The birds will soon fly high again.
Have a good look. Can you see all TEN?